Mystery of the Attic

By: TJ Perkins

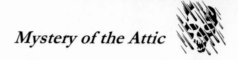

Second printing

ISBN 0-9777538-6-7
(previously ISBN 1-59286-768-5)
Published by GumShoe Press
www.authorsden.com/tjperkins

Order more copies of the
Kim & Kelly Mystery Series
From Ingram, Bowker, Books in Print,
or your favorite distributor

Printed in the United States of America

The location and house in this story is real, only the names of people and streets have been changed. The house still stands today and the new owners said they have never seen or heard anything unusual since they moved in.

This book is dedicated to anyone that's had a really scary experience and couldn't get anybody to believe you!

Mystery of the Attic

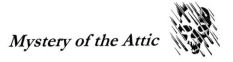

More Mysteries by TJ Perkins

FANTASIES ARE MURDER

THE SECRET IN PHANTOM FOREST

TRADE SECRET

IMAGE IN THE TAPESTRY

WOUND TOO TIGHT

MYSTERY OF THE ATTIC

ON FORBIDDEN GROUND

Through the swirling cloud the shape of a hideous skull came into view. It scowled at me and its mouth was twisted into an evil grin. It started growing and filling the whole doorway.

CHAPTER 1

*M*oving can be hard on most kids, but not me. It seemed like we moved once a year to one small country town or another - bouncing back and forth between the state lines of Maryland and Pennsylvania. When you move so much, at a very young age, you get used to it; it just becomes a way of life. We didn't have much money and always lived in old drafty farmhouses with a dirt road a mile long for a driveway - ten thousand miles away from anyone.

Being an only child and growing up in such isolated places wasn't a big thrill but I learned to entertain myself...as most young girls do. My mom worked all the time and my dad was never around. When Dad was around, all he and Mom did was fight. Years later, it didn't surprise me when Mom announced that they were getting a divorce. After a few years she married a man named Don. He and his daughter, Becky, came to live with us but our place was too small. So we had to move - again.

Moving this time wasn't so bad, many of my cousins and my favorite uncle, Steve, lived close by. We were still in the farming area of New Windsor, Maryland, which was still too far from my friends, but I could deal with that. The house was just a few miles down the street from our old house and I could continue going to the same school with the same kids. My routine wouldn't get jostled around too much.

Mom drove me to the house we were moving into early one morning and I was totally fascinated by what I saw. Our new house was actually on a huge plot of land that used to be a fully functional farm, but it was really old with rundown buildings that nobody used anymore. I was intrigued with the fact that it had been built back in the late 1800's and my mind raced with ideas of what it used to look like back in its prime. The house was big and oddly shaped and the neatest house I'd ever seen. It was three stories high and solid brick with huge, narrow windows. The wood that bordered the windows, doors and the roof wasn't in very good condition due to the fact that you could see splintered wood and peeling paint from a distance. There was a door on three different sides of the house; front, side and back. There were also three windows at the very top, under the roof, giving light to the attic. Above each window, the roof was shaped into a point and reminded me of a big triangle. I wondered to myself if there was a particular reason for the number three, but let the notion go and didn't give it another thought.

"Melissa, go on inside and pick out your room," Mom said with a slight nod of her head toward the house, "but grab something on your way in." Her face was turning bright red as she struggled with more than an arm-full of clothes.

"Let me take some of those." I suggested, lifting a small bundle from her arms. I happily trotted up the long, concrete sidewalk on my way to the front door, passing a porch that went almost totally around the house. Once I got to the entrance something made me stop and look up at the big windows at the top of the house. I don't know why, I just felt compelled to look up. As I stood staring at the attic windows, I suddenly felt a cold chill run up my spine and the hair on my arms instantly stood up. I shook it off and stumbled on a loose floorboard as I entered the kitchen, which lightened the moment and made me laugh at myself for being such a klutz. The kitchen was huge and I slowed my pace while gazing over the layout. A long porcelain sink inhabited an entire wall, a modern stove was in the center of the room with an island attached to it, and lots of cabinets and closets filled another wall. I was half way across the kitchen when I started to get another weird feeling. It was as though a weight was pressing against me, or someone was looking over my shoulder. I turned around in a circle, while searching the room with my eyes. No one was there. I then noticed a stairway next to the far wall of the kitchen and decided to see where it led.

The stairway curved sharply at the bottom, and then straightened out all the way up to the top of the second floor. When I reached the second floor I saw many doors. The three doors on the right opened to standard sized bedrooms with adjoining doors and very tiny closets. To my left was a large, long bathroom and then, next to that, I passed through a big room that led to two other rooms on either side of it.

"This is going to be my room," A voice said, making me nearly jump out of my skin.

"Becky, how long have you been here?" I tried my best not to sound upset with her. She was two years younger and she loved to pester me. Her Dad was now my step-Dad, which made her my stepsister. We got along, most of the time, but there were those times when she tried to show that she was smarter than me. It would eat right through me. To top it all off, she was prettier than me. She was tall and slim, with shiny, straight blonde hair that hung down to her backside. It was thick and never looked limp or messy. She even had perfect skin, perfect nails, - perfect everything!

Then there was me; mousy blonde hair that hung to my shoulder blades, stringy, limp and lifeless no matter what I did to it. I was getting zits and I always experimented with make-up, trying to cover

12

them up and trying to make myself attractive. I was skinny too, but more athletically built. I already had the budding features of a woman and all the problems a thirteen year old could possibly have.

"I've been waiting for you. Which room do you want?" she asked, cocking her head to the side with a girlish smile.

"This one looks okay," I replied, walking into the room located on the left and dropping the clothes on the floor. "The only problem is, I'll have to keep cutting through your room to get to it. Hope you don't mind."

"What can I do? Mom and Dad will have to do the same thing to get to their room, too," she said with a giggle at her smart remark.

"Mom wants us to help bring some stuff in, but I want to look around real quick. Wanna come?" I said. Her face brightened as she lightly bounced in front of me, leading the way into the room adjacent to hers.

"Here, let me show you. This is going to be our parents' room," she said, happily displaying how much more she already knew than I did. "And look," she added with excitement, "here's another door that leads back out into the hallway. See…it makes a complete circle." She swung it open and I stepped out into the end of the hallway and immediately noticed that to my right, there was another door.

"Where does this go?"

"I dunno," Becky said, shrugging her shoulders.

13

Here was a twist -something Becky didn't know. A smug smile appeared on my face. Leaning slightly to my left I could see straight down the hallway to the top of the steps I had just climbed coming up from the kitchen. Down the left side of the hallway were the three bedrooms I had just looked at, and directly behind me was a huge window.

"This has to be the attic," I finally deducted. "Wanna check it out?" My hand reached for the old fashioned latch-lock.

CHAPTER 2

"*G*irls!" Mom shouted. Her voice made me jerk my hand away from the latch and for some odd reason my heart was pounding. "Get down here and finish helping me!" She was beginning to sound angry and on a warm day like today I could see why.

"Becky, Melissa!" Dad chimed in, "You'd better listen!"

"Oh no, the old threat…" Becky mocked quietly, turning away from me and starting down the hall and apparently loosing interest in exploring the attic with me.

"Yeah, but he doesn't just threaten, he delivers," I commented, following her.

We totally forgot about the attic and finished moving our stuff in, and spent the rest of the week getting settled and arranging our rooms.

Life went along at a nice, easy pace. Becky and I still fought about stupid stuff once in a while. We basically had the same interests and liked the same things, but that still didn't stop us from chewing each other's heads off. Every other weekend she would have to visit her mom and that gave us a break from each other.

We'd only been in our new house for two months when the weather started changing. It was getting colder and we could really feel how drafty this old house was going to be. I had to pile lots of blankets on my bed because the cold air literally seeped right through the walls and windows and no amount of whining was going to get Mom to turn up the heat. So, I suffered night after night, freezing until the bed got warm, listening to the wind howling outside, the branches hitting together and something that kept scratching on my window every time the wind blew. Then one night, I heard noises in the walls. The first time I heard them Becky and Dad weren't home. I had just gone to bed and it was very quiet upstairs. Then the scratching sounds began. Like tiny pin pricks on wood they would start off faint then grow with intensity and fade away again.

At first I just remained very still, my eyes searching the darkness of my room, trying to pinpoint where the sounds were coming from. When there was a pause accompanied by silence, I rolled over onto my stomach and stared at the wall behind my bed. Then it started up again, but now something was running back and forth inside the wall. As I listened closely it became apparent that there was more than one kind of *something*. Then the sounds would stop and be replaced by scratching and chewing noises getting louder and closer. It seemed like *it* was trying to get out! What if it chewed right through the wall while I was sleeping and crawled all over me? Maybe chewing on me?!

I leaped out of bed and hurried down the stairs, almost slipping on the curve near the bottom.

"Mom, there's something in my room." It was a small exaggeration devised to get her attention. She was lying on the couch in front of the TV almost ready to nod off when she awoke with a start.

"Melissa!" She practically shouted sitting up and rubbing her eyes, "What's the problem?"

"Sorry, there's something chewing and clawing at the wall behind my bed." I put on the best upset look I could muster so that I could win her sympathy. It worked.

"Okay, show me," she said, getting up and stomping to the stairway.

"Well, do you have to be so loud? You might scare it away and then you'll never hear it or believe me," I whined. Rolling her eyes she followed me into my room. We sat quietly together in the dark, on the edge of my bed and waited for the sounds to begin again. It didn't take long for the entertainment to start.

"Oh, for goodness sake, it's just mice!" She said,

annoyed. "Melissa, they're not going to come out and get you. They're more afraid of you than you are of them. Now cut it out and go to sleep. There's nothing to be afraid of." She rambled on as she walked away, cutting through Becky's room to her own, "You're too old be acting like a baby." I was glad Becky wasn't in her bed to hear Mom say that. She was at her Mom's for the weekend and Dad, a pipeline engineer, was away working. Sometimes he was gone for months.

"Oh, well," I sighed to myself, "so now I have to deal with this noise all winter long." At that moment I heard a quiet giggle coming from somewhere in my room; soft and child-like it was something so bizarre that you would almost swear you were imagining things and ignore it, but I just had to double check with my Mom and make sure I wasn't going nuts.

"Mom, did you laugh about something?" I asked.

"No."

Hmmm, very strange.

CHAPTER 3

I heard another noise one night while Dad and Becky were gone. I was in bed and it was getting late when the sound started. It wasn't just any kind of common house sound and it wasn't the mice, this one was different, very distinct and unmistakable. I heard footsteps, no, more like shoes or maybe, boots. Yes, that was it, but from where? I held my breath, not wanting to disrupt the racket, and strained my ears to pinpoint the location. The attic! Whoa, something, or someone is walking around up there!

I shook my head from side to side to make sure I wasn't dreaming, and then I looked up to the ceiling, blinked my eyes and pinched my arm to make absolutely sure I was awake.

"Ouch!" Yep, I was awake and I was definitely hearing footsteps. Then as suddenly as they began, they stopped. I waited for what seemed like forever but I heard nothing.

"This is ridiculous," I muttered to myself, "This is not possible. There's no way someone is up there."

I jumped out of bed, cut through Becky's room and came to a sliding halt out in the hallway. Rising up on the balls of my feet I tried to walk softly; I didn't want any boards to creak, which might give away my position to the mystery trespasser in the attic. I made my way to the beginning of the long stretch of hall that led to the attic door and peered into the darkness. There was a pole-light on that side of the house and its light was shining through the large hall window.

"I could go right down the hall to the attic door," I thought. The pole-light will brighten everything up and I won't have to turn on all the lights and make Mom mad. I began taking slow, cautious steps down the hall, while trying to control the shaking in my legs and my pounding heart. All the while my mind was racing, speculating, that maybe what was in the attic was a ghost, a lost soul, or something evil. I stopped halfway down the hall and for the first time heard the TV running. Mom was asleep again in front of the TV. She's been doing that a lot lately - ever since we moved in.

I abandoned the idea of checking out the attic and decided to go downstairs and get Mom to bed. Besides, I would feel better knowing she was upstairs with me. The only thing I didn't like was the fact that the attic door was right outside her room. What if something got her in the middle of the night and then came to get me?

"You really have to stop this," I said to myself, *"there is nothing in this house. You're letting your imagination run away with you. Get a grip! Tomorrow at school I'll go to the library and get books about this kind of stuff. The best way to fight something is to understand it."* With those words of wisdom in my head, I continued down stairs to get Mom.

The next morning, while Mom was getting ready for work and I was getting ready for school, I decided to talk to her about what had happened.

"I swear to you, it really happened, I heard it." I was trying my best to get Mom to believe me, but was getting nowhere fast.

"Yes, Melissa, of course, if you say so," She humored me, trying her best to hide her laughter. She didn't do a very good job at hiding it and I was really getting frustrated. She was always so down-to-earth and practical, so serious and logical.

"Mom," I argued, my words getting tight in my throat, "why won't you believe me?"

"It's not that at all," She said, using her sympathetic voice.

"Then what?" I came back, slamming down my comb and knocking the toothpaste tube onto the floor.

"That's enough, young lady!" Her voice had taken on an edge and that meant I'd gone a bit too far. The toothpaste tube found its way back to the bathroom counter in Mom's hand, with a hard *slam*. She put away her makeup and finished fluffing her short, dark brown hair then turned sharply toward me. I felt myself shrink back under her gaze and quickly made myself busy by tucking my shirt into my jeans.

"Get your school stuff and hurry to the end of the driveway for the bus to pick you up. We'll talk about this another time and when we do, it will not be a debate."

So, that was that. 'Ms. Logical' wasn't going to buy my story. Nothing more was said as she gave me a quick kiss good-bye on the cheek and left for work, leaving me to catch the bus by myself, which was no big deal. Half way down the driveway I stopped and looked back at the house and the three huge windows at the top. I wondered if, perhaps, someone was watching me from the attic.

There was no way I could tell because the sun was shining on the windows and mirroring the tall pine trees that surrounded the house. I shook my head, disgusted at myself for thinking so crazy, but just as I turned away my eyes caught a faint glimpse of a figure moving by the hallway window. I froze and stared at the window, trying to make sure that I saw what I thought I saw but there was no more movement.

"That's the window right outside the attic door," I whispered to myself. The compulsion to turn around and go back to the house seized my gut, but the sound of the school bus coming down the road forced me to give up. That was okay, there was always later when I got home.

CHAPTER 4

I was the first one home in the afternoon and couldn't wait to search the house. When I found no trace of anyone or anything mysterious, I just sat down and did my homework. Mom came home two hours after me and Becky's Mom dropped her off after dinner. I was actually glad when Becky finally came home and I couldn't wait to tell her about the past happenings once we were up in my room in secret.

"You're kidding me," Becky said, eyes wide with excitement and disbelief, she almost half whispered her words. "This is so excellent."

"I'm not lying, I'm very, very serious," I summed up with a very determined look on my face, after filling her in on all of the sinister events. "And I got all these books from the library. I'm going to read up on weird stuff like this, that way, if this ever

24

happens again, hopefully I'll be prepared to deal with it."

"Can I read too?" She asked.

"Sure." I was happy to have an ally, even though she did get on my nerves at times.

Later that night we lay awake in our beds waiting for the walking sound to happen, but it never did. In fact, I didn't hear it again for weeks. Believe it or not, I was actually disappointed. Then I remembered an old saying that goes, when you least expect it, expect it. Boy, was that the truth. Weeks later, when Becky was gone and Dad was still away working, the walking sound happened again.

It started out so loud it jolted me out of a sound sleep! I sat up in bed listening intently to the echoing sounds. First it walked to the front of the house then to the back. It lasted a long time and I was very excited.

"I've got to get Mom so she can hear this," I said to myself, but as soon as I made it to the hallway everything stopped. I waited to see if it would start up again, but it didn't. Hesitantly, I started back to my room when I heard a shuffling of feet down the hall and a door shut. I whirled around hoping to catch a glimpse of the culprit, but there was no one there.

The three empty bedrooms down the left side of the hallway had their doors closed because Mom and Dad just used them for storage instead of putting stuff in the attic. Dad wanted to keep the

25

doors closed so he could shut off the heat on that side of the house to conserve energy. It sounded like a great idea since no one was using the bedrooms, but now someone had gone into one of them. It was hard to tell which one, but I had to try and figure it out. The house was so still and quiet I could've heard a pin drop, a creaking board, or anything. I stood with my feet apart and arms crossed over my chest, surveying the task before me. I was determined to get to the bottom of this.

I decided to turn on the hall light. Then I opened each door, in turn, stepping into the first room and then the second room, listening and quickly searching the emptiness with my eyes. There was nothing in the first two rooms, but I still had one more to go and it was at the end of the hall - next to the attic door. The hair on the back of my neck bristled and a chill ran up my spine as I neared the door. It felt as if someone was watching me, and it almost seemed like a presence was pressing against me. I paused outside the door and spun around, expecting to find someone *or something* behind me. Nothing. Turning my attention back to the door, I reached for the old-fashioned latch with trembling hands. I stared intently at the latch as my hand inched closer, hesitating then moving forward. My heart was beating wildly; I could feel the pounding in my head and I had to constantly lick my drying lips. What if there *is* someone in here? But what if they've snuck out through one of the adjoining doors and into the other rooms I've already checked? Swallowing past a lump in my throat and taking a deep breath I made up my mind to do it, to grab that latch and swing the door open.

"Melissa!" Mom's voice startled me right out of my skin, leaving me trembling and breathing so hard I had to put a hand to my chest. "What are you doing? It's eleven o'clock at night." She definitely knocked a few good years off my life. She scared me to death! I turned my head to look at her and my eyes were wide with panic. Mom was standing at the other end of the hall by the bathroom with a very bewildered look on her face.

"Mom, I swear, someone was in the hall and went into one of these rooms. I checked the other two and no one was in them ---," I blurted out and was quickly cut off.

"Well, of course no one was in those rooms. No one else is in this house but you and I. Now will you please stop all this nonsense!" She began raising her voice with every breath she took as she started coming toward me.

"Okay, fine, I'll prove it. Just look!" I said, grabbing the latch and throwing the door open. She stepped into the room next to me and turned on the light. In just a flash I thought I saw a shadow move on the wall and heard faint whispering.

"Well?" She demanded.

"I'm not making this up. Believe me, I have better things to do than to create delusions." I plundered through a convincing explanation as she closed up the room, turned off all the lights and ushered me to my bedroom.

"Get some sleep and I don't want any more of this *'someone's in the house'* stuff," she mumbled, as she shuffled to her room and turned out the light. I climbed into bed but was unable to sleep. The quiet harmony of the winter evening took over. I lay awake, listening to the wind rustle the leaves around outside.

"Maybe that's what I really heard in the hall, sometimes sounds play tricks on the mind," I muttered quietly to myself. It was then that I heard the soft giggle again. It was a boy's giggle coming from one of the posters in my room. "It wasn't funny," I said very tight-lipped, yet in a quiet voice. I was nervous about talking to the giggle and felt like I should stay very still. "Show yourself to me," I demanded, but all that I got was another soft giggle and then...silence.

CHAPTER 5

*T*he next day I helped Mom clean the house. It didn't take me very long to finish my chores and when I was done I had the rest of the day to do whatever I wanted. After last night's incident there was only one thing on my mind and I quickly went to work.

Sitting Indian-style in the center of my bed, I spread all of my books out and began flipping through the ones on restless spirits and unexplained phenomenon. Then I heard the giggle again. This time it happened in the middle of the day and it was very clear that I wasn't imagining it.

"Who's there?" I asked very sternly, my eyes darting around the room. The giggle came again. "Stop this craziness and talk to me."

"You won't find your answers in a book," the voice said.

"Why not?" I asked nervously, trying not to panic. I really didn't think I was actually going to get an answer to my demand and wasn't sure how to handle it.

"Because all the answers you need are right here in this house," the voice stated.

Just then I heard three loud pounding sounds, like someone pounding on wood with their fist, up in the attic.

"He doesn't want me to talk to you," the voice explained.

"He?" I questioned. "Who is *he*? Why doesn't *he* want you talking to me?"

"Because he's afraid you'll set my spirit to rest and he will be alone and angry forever." The boy's voice trailed off as the walking in the attic began.

This was it, the chance I had been waiting for, ever since I first heard the strange walking in the attic. I actually had a ghost talking to me, giving me some answers and because of that the haunting in the attic finally started up again. Now was a perfect opportunity to see who, or what, was making this racket and hopefully put an end to it. I had to admit that curiosity and my determination to find out the originator of the noise got the better of me in just a matter of minutes. There was no way I was going to chicken out now.

"Well, we'll just have to have a talk with this person and end all this mess," I stated to the voice, while bounding off my bed and cutting through Becky's room. Suddenly, I began feeling heaviness in my chest and thighs. It was making my breath come in little gasps and I could hardly walk, or pick up my feet.

"No!" The voice cut into my mind, "Don't do it! You have no idea what you're dealing with."

I stopped out in the hall. The clomping sound was really loud and nonstop.

"Melissa," Mom called up to me, "Who are you talking to?"

Oh, this was too perfect. "Mom, come up here, quick, quick," I whispered, waving her on and looking up at the ceiling. She trotted up the stairs as the noise in the attic was still going on and I was incredibly happy that she would finally get to hear the very thing I'd been telling her about.

"Shhh, stop right there and listen," I whispered, pausing, looking into her face and smiling. She smiled back at me with a confused look on her face.

"What?" she questioned, "What am I suppose to hear?"

"Awww, Mom. Don't you hear it?" I asked, looking up at the ceiling.

"Hear what?" Was all I got from her.

I stared at her with my mouth hanging open and released a sigh of defeat. I couldn't believe it! Here we were, standing together, the walking in the attic was going full force with loud, stomping and clomping sounds and I was the only one who could hear it! Why can't she hear it? This was crazy!

"Melissa, hear what?" Mom asked again.

I was about to answer when the sound stopped. I

31

let out another deep sigh and shook my head, "N-nothing. It was nothing. I-it was probably just mice again," I finally stammered.

"Oh, all right then. Is there anything else you don't want me to hear?" she joked.

"Very funny," I smirked as she went back downstairs laughing to herself and shaking her head.

It was quite obvious I was on my own. Maybe only kids could hear the walking sounds? Maybe Becky will be able to hear it?

I went back to my room and sat heavily on the edge of the bed. I was pondering all kinds of things in my head when it felt like someone was looking over my shoulder. I stood up and whirled around in one motion, but no one was there. Then I remembered my unseen visitor.

"Are you here?" I asked into the air.

"Yes," the boy answered.

"Do you have a name?" I asked.

"Josh," he said.

"Okay, Josh, let's get to the bottom of this. First of all, what did you do to me out there?" I demanded, pointing in the direction of the hallway, "and second, who are you and what's the connection with you and this walking in the attic thing?" There was a pause. I crossed my arms over my chest and tapped my foot. "Josh, please, in this life time."

"Well, I, ah, I had to stop you, Melissa," he stammered, "I have a hard time touching living things, but I *am* getting better. Hope I didn't hurt you."

His last words were very apologetic and it made me feel like I was being too hard on him.

"No, you didn't. It just felt weird. But I need you to tell me everything." I sat down again on my bed Indian-style and waited for him to spill the whole story.

"This house was built back in the late 1800's, my Mom and I, as well as three other people, were servants here. The man who owned this house had two daughters and a young son. His son, William, was really nasty and when their mother died William became evil. He was always trying to make accidents happen to his sisters, you know, like really trying to hurt them or maybe even kill them. His father and sisters didn't have a clue that he was behind the accidents because he always lied. Well, I caught him setting up several schemes and he beat me up in the basement lots of times. He threatened to kill me if I told."

"That's terrible!" I exclaimed, "Sorry, I didn't mean to interrupt."

"Anyway, I also found out that his mother had a box full of jewelry that was worth a lot of money. His father kept it in what's now your parents' room, locked away. Apparently, the sisters didn't realize that their father was very sick. Of course the old rule of the family was that if he died the fortune would go to the oldest, which would've been the sister. Well, one day, I caught William sneaking around again. He had taken the box of jewelry and buried it in the wall in the basement."

"What do you mean by 'buried'?" I asked, just wanting to clarify the vision I was getting from the story.

"He dug a hole in the wall, put the box of jewelry in the hole, and then plastered it up. I confronted him about what he did and I threatened to tell his father, but before I got a chance he snuck up to our rooms, which were in the attic, and poisoned me."

"Poisoned you!"

"Yes. We were getting ready to have a late supper and the food was sitting unattended for a brief moment. After I ate I felt really sick. William came up to check on me, acting like he really cared, and as I lay in bed he leaned close to my ear and admitted that he poisoned me. I was too weak and sick to say or do anything. My mind was screaming but I didn't have the strength to tell anyone. I couldn't move my mouth. I just laid there feeling my life slip away."

"That's horrible," I said quietly. "So, why are you still here?"

"I guess it's because I died an unjust death. So, I figured out that I need someone to tell the truth about my death and find the family fortune. It really should be returned to any living family member."

"But I have no proof..." I started, but was quickly cut off by Josh's over-excitement.

"I'm going to help you with that. But before I

do, you must promise not to confront William's spirit."

"Why? Is he stuck in the attic?" I said, mockingly.

"Yes," Josh said, flatly.

"Wait a minute," I said, picking up one of my books and flipping the pages. I stopped at a paragraph I had marked. "It says here, a spirit can only come into your house or world if you invite it in. Hmm, I guess that would mean, like opening a door for it, huh?"

"Please say you won't do that," Josh pleaded.

"Look, if I do, and he comes down, then we can have a big show down."

"No, Melissa, no. You have no idea what you're up against," Josh's voice wavered and he sounded like he was ready to cry.

"All right, Josh, don't freak out on me."

"Melissa," Suddenly he sounded far away, "I need you to help me. I don't want anything to happen to you." His voice trailed off and I suddenly felt alone in my room. I waited for him to say something.

"Josh?" I called. "Josh, what happened?" Silence. This was too weird.

CHAPTER 6

I was awakened from a deep sleep, by the sound of walking in the attic. I lay there, wondering if I was dreaming, listening to the steady clomping above me as the footsteps repeatedly went from one side of the house to the other and thinking of all the things Josh had said to me earlier in the day. It was William, that much was clear, and as far as I was concerned his constant vigil to irritate me was quickly coming to an end. He'd made me look like a fool one too many times in front of my Mom and I wasn't going to put up with his nightly disturbances any longer. I wasn't easily defeated and - unfortunately for William - I was very hard headed.

It was dark and quiet upstairs as I stepped out into the hallway. The wood floor was cold on my bare feet and I welcomed it. It reminded me that I was awake and alive and doing something I really had no business doing. The only light to guide me down the long dark hall came from the pole-light shining in the hallway window. The walking sounds were very loud and gave the impression that they were angry, but I continued to slowly pad down the long stretch of hallway that led to the attic door.

I could hear the TV still on downstairs and I knew Mom was asleep on the sofa again. That was fine; at least she was far away from the situation. The tramping upstairs was becoming louder and more aggressive with every step I took toward the attic door. I rose up on the balls of my feet, trying to be as quiet as I could. It seemed like the angry footsteps knew my exact position. They were mad, pounding the ceiling with hard, determined steps. The sound was echoing in my head by the time I made it halfway down the hall.

My heart was racing as I came to my destination and I peeked slightly around the wall until I could see the attic door laying flush to the edge. My nose was so close to the crack of the doorjamb that I could feel a slight draft coming through. Without warning, the angry footsteps came pounding down the attic steps and stopped on the other side of the door. There was a deadly silence that followed and it made my blood run cold as I stepped directly in front of the entry and contemplated the next move. But whose move? Mine? Or the angry spirit's?

Should I open it? Should I invite *it* in? I could

confront this being once and for all. Or could I? My curiosity was heightened. It was there, just on the other side of this portal. I could just reach out and lift the latch, I could see what it was, what it looked like. I honestly didn't even know if I wanted to see what it looked like but this silence after the parade of loud footsteps was really getting to me. I just felt that I needed to initiate the first move.

For some reason, I wasn't afraid as I reached for the latch. My hand didn't shake and I was very calm. In fact, I felt like laughing and a cluster of quiet giggles escaped from my mouth, but only for a brief moment for the sound of a pounding fist from behind the other side of the door jerked me back to reality. I stood, frozen in space and time, staring at the entrance to the attic. There was a slight pause and more pounding. It really wanted out and it knew I was here to set it free.

My hand dropped to my side, I couldn't do this, this was wrong, all wrong. Just when I was about to back away I suddenly heard a sniffing noise; a deep, long, repeated sniffing noise. Something was sniffing all around the doorjamb and threshold and it sounded BIG!

My mind pictured a big, hairy creature, like a werewolf or something and it sensed I was there. It could smell me, smell my fear, I just knew it. The sniffing was then replaced by a scratching and clawing sound and it didn't take long for the clawing to quicken, becoming more determined and excited with every movement. I finally took a step back, trying to get a better view of the entire door. What was I to do? Where could I possibly go? The clawing was just a sound, right? It couldn't get out unless I invited it, right? Or maybe it would just burst out anyway and rip me to shreds!

The pole-light from outside lit up the whole scene and everything was very clear. As the clawing continued I could see the bottom corner of the door, the weakest part, begin to shudder under the unseen force.

"Oh no," I whispered to myself, "It's gonna come out whether it's invited or not." I took several steps backward and hid next to the edge of the wall. From this position I could still see what was happening but felt a measure of safety.

The clawing suddenly ceased and, after a brief pause, was replaced by something I never thought possible. It seemed that the thing behind the attic door was pressing all its weight against the door, the only barrier keeping it in and me safe. I stared intently as I watched the door begin to warp under a tremendous strain. It began to bow slightly, in and out, in and out, each time bending outwards just a little bit more until I heard the wood start to crack and splinter.

That was enough for me! I turned and ran down the hallway and downstairs. I rushed into the living room to see Mom asleep on the sofa. Still able to hear the noise upstairs, I grabbed her by the arm and shook her.

"Mom! Get up!" I shouted, "Mom, please,

there isn't much time." She wouldn't move. She just snorted and rolled over.

"Now what?" I asked out loud, "Josh, where are you?"

I was beginning to panic, I had nowhere to run, nowhere to go, Mom was totally comatose on the sofa and I was alone. I could run out into the cold, dark night but the nearest neighbor was a quarter of a mile away! Besides, by the time I got back with help Mom would probably be torn apart by that thing from the attic. This was all my fault! If I hadn't been so hard headed and listened to Josh this wouldn't be happening. I had to deal with it, I had to set things right - some how.

I could hear the attic door groaning under the force of whatever was behind it, pushing tirelessly and relentlessly with supernatural strength. My feet had led me back upstairs and I stood in the center of the hall looking down to the end and listening to all the commotion. At a loss for what to do next, or how to stop it, I panicked and ran into my room, jumped into bed and pulled the covers up over my head. Then, in an instant, everything stopped. It was the weirdest thing; the noise stopped exactly when I had pulled the covers up over my head. The house was silent and still, as if I had dreamt it all.

Realizing I had been holding my breath, I started to breathe again. My whole body was trembling and I was too afraid to remove the covers from my head. What if that thing was in my room, looming over me, waiting to tear my face off? But I couldn't stay like this forever. Slowly, bravely, I pulled down the blankets and took a relaxing breath. Nothing was there. Then I heard Mom turn on the hall light and start up the stairs. What if it was out in the hall waiting to pounce on her? Nothing happened as I listened to her heavy footsteps heading toward her room. I sat up in bed. Had I dreamt it? No. I was there. I saw everything. I felt the cold floor on my feet and felt the pounding in my head. There was no mistaking it, it had actually happened and I had survived.

What if this was just a sample of what was to come if I continued to talk to Josh and help him? Maybe I should promise William that I won't help Josh? But that would be unfair to him after I agreed to help and besides I couldn't let this spirit intimidate me. I lay back down and snuggled into my blankets, took a deep breath and tried to go to sleep.

From somewhere in my room a deep, breathy voice shattered my slowly settling nerves.

"Beware," it whispered and then there was total silence. It made my skin crawl and my mouth go dry and didn't make going to sleep any easier.

CHAPTER 7

*B*ecky came home from her Mom's house early the next day. I couldn't wait to tell her my story but decided that it should be told in secrecy. I convinced her to put on her coat and take a walk with me to the old barn and some of the old buildings we liked to explore.

"So, what's the big secret?" She asked, once we were comfortable in the barn. "Why'd you want to come out here? It's freezing. Did you do something behind Mom's back?" Her questions were getting on my nerves and I really wanted her to shut up.

"Shhhh," I said quickly, "No, it's nothing like that. It's the happenings in the house."

"Again! Awww, man, why does everything happen when I'm gone?" She wailed.

"You know what," I said, sitting on a hay bale and petting one of our fifteen barn cats, "that's a very good question."

She sat down next to me. "All right, fill me in," she said, scooping up a gray and white cat, which she held for a moment until it jumped down and was joined by five other barn cats swirling around our legs.

As I filled her in, she listened quietly, pulling her knees close to her chest for warmth and resting her chin on them as even more cats gathered around us for attention.

I told her all the bone chilling details about the night before as she sat with wide eyes, hanging onto every word.

"Of course after all that's happened, I felt it was best to discuss this outside the house. I don't want that spirit to hear us talking," I explained.

"Yeah, who knows what it'll do next. But we really have to help Josh," she agreed.

"I don't know how we're going to get proof that Josh was poisoned, but the first thing we're going to do is find that box of jewelry in the basement," I said in a determined voice. "Dad has all kinds of tools that we can use. And if we talk to some of the elderly neighbors I'm sure someone will know the name of the family that lived here."

"And maybe someone knows where to find their relatives," Becky put in. "I think we should do that first."

I stood up, stretched and brushed the hay off my bottom. "Let's get going. We have to do everything very quickly, before the spirit of William has a

43

chance to think of doing anything to us."

"Lead on," Becky said, gesturing for me to walk ahead of her. "I can't wait to hear what you've cooked up as an excuse to interrogate our neighbors."

With our neighbors being so far away, we only made it to three houses. We wound up having long talks with the elderly people in each home. After I explained that we were working on a school project and needed their comments, they were full of answers. Each story was slightly different but all led in the same direction. Becky took notes as I interviewed each person and we quickly began to realize that a genuine plot was beginning to form.

The last neighbor we visited was an elderly lady named Miss Summers. Becky and I sat in her cozy, old fashioned sitting room and intently listened to her spin a yarn about days gone by. At this point we were very excited because we found out she was a great granddaughter of the oldest sister of the family that had lived in the house.

"I used to think the stories my great grandmother told me weren't true," She said in a tired, shaky voice. She paused to gingerly take a sip of tea, waited a moment and then began again, "She told me about the death of the young servant boy. No one knew what caused it. His mother went to her grave thinking it was her fault. And then the death of her brother, William, just the next day, oh my," She trailed off with a sad little chuckle.

"What do you mean? Her brother died the next day?" I asked.

"Well, you see," Miss Summers took another sip of tea and sat the cup on a little table next to her. She looked at both of us then laid her hands together on her lap. "It's like this girls," she said, very matter-of-factly, "her brother, William, had become very disturbed after their mother died. My great grandmother used to say that she felt like he was out to kill her and her sister. Why, the very night the servant boy died, William had brought her a cup of tea and for some odd reason was trying his best to get her to drink it right away. Once she heard all the fuss in the servants' quarters upstairs the tea was forgotten, left on the table next to another cup. Later, when they returned to the sitting room, one of the servants had prepared more tea. Now several cups sat together on the table. William mistakenly took a sip from the cup that was meant for his sister."

"Then he died a short time afterwards, huh?" Becky chimed in. Miss Summers shook her head slowly in agreement.

"My great grandmother swore she saved that tea," Miss Summers said with a twinkle in her eye.

"What did she do with it?" I asked, practically sitting on the edge of my chair.

"I was told she put it in a tiny perfume bottle and hid it in the house." Miss Summers finished her story and leaned back into her rocking chair, closing her eyes. She was silent for a short while and

Becky and I were a bit confused. We weren't sure if she fell asleep or if that was our hint to leave, but presently she spoke up, adding a bit more to her story, "Their father was so upset over the death of William that he died of heart failure a few weeks later. The daughters couldn't afford to stay in the house because the family fortune was missing, so they sold it and moved away."

I could see that Becky was ready to leap out of her seat and dash down the road to our house so we thanked Miss Summers and left.

"Now we have to find two things," Becky complained as we hurried home.

"We can do it you know, you and me, and nothing is going to stop us," I said very determined.

"We'll give the jewelry to Miss Summers once we find it," Becky stated.

"Yep," I agreed, "and then we'll get the poison analyzed and put a statement in the newspaper telling the real story of what happened."

"*If* we find it you mean. We have to do everything at the same time you know, one right after the other," Becky reminded me.

"Yeah, that's going to be the hard part." I let out a deep sigh as the whole process weighed heavily on my mind.

CHAPTER 8

"*K*eep going!" I complained as Becky stopped abruptly in front of me for the fourth time.

"It's really dark down here Melissa. Why don't you go first?" Becky whined. We stumbled down the old basement steps; the light by the entrance wasn't enough to see the steps at the bottom.

"Well, okay." I gave in with a heavy sigh and inched past Becky. I adjusted the high-powered flashlight that I had been holding high above my head and cradled several tools we could use to hack through the old concrete walls, compliments of our Dad who had no idea we had borrowed them.

"Dad's going to bust our butts if he catches us doing this," Becky worried out loud.

"Look, we agreed to do this as quickly as possible, we just need to find a spot that looks different from the rest of the wall. You know, something slightly newer than the rest of the wall. This house was standing a long time before William sealed up the jewelry case and the spot on the wall has to be different." I kept talking as we walked through the basement. The sound of my voice made my heart stand still. Becky, on the other hand, wasn't holding up too good. She was shaking so badly that she had a hard time holding her flashlight still.

"Calm down, okay, it'll be all right. Trust me," I said to her, with a reassuring smile and placing a hand on her shoulder.

"Yeah, all right," she breathed each word out heavily.

The basement wound around under the house, creating separate small rooms that joined to one another. It smelled musty and cobwebs hung in abundance from the wooden ceiling. We tried our best to ignore the darkness that seemed to surround us as we shuffled along the dirt floor, while closely scanning the walls.

"Maybe we should split up," Becky suggested.

"If we do William might attack one of us. You know, divide and conquer," I reminded her, "That is why we are doing this together instead of me doing this and you looking for the bottle of tea with poison in it."

"Well, let's hurry this up," she continued to complain.

I didn't say anymore. We had gone all the way around the basement and were approaching the area where we had begun our search in the first place. Becky was slightly ahead of me, scanning the walls with a bit less concern than I was.

"Melissa," she suddenly whispered, "I think I found something."

Sure enough, she had found a spot on the wall that looked different from the rest of the plaster.

I quickly began chipping away at the spot. Becky felt the best approach was to start around the edges but I just went right for the center. We were really into what we were doing but for some odd reason an uneasiness crept up on me and I stopped several times to look over my shoulder, squinting my eyes into the darkness that surrounded us.

"What?" Becky asked, noticing my actions.

"I dunno," I replied quietly, "I keep thinking I hear someone coming down the steps." We both shrugged and continued hacking at the wall. The plaster fell away quickly once we removed the outer layer, allowing Becky to reach into the hole with both hands, clawing the remaining plaster away and revealing an old brown box.

"This is it!" She exclaimed, removing a small, flat box from its hiding place and hugging it close to her chest.

"What are you two doing!" Dad shouted angrily. We spun around to face him, startled and shaking in our shoes. He stomped down the basement steps and came toward us.

"Dad, I can explain," I stammered, but never had the chance to finish.

"Look at the mess you've made! Now I'll have to fix it!"

"We were just exploring and we saw a hole there and thought something was in it," Becky tried her best to blurt out a lie but Dad grabbed us by our arms and shoved us toward the steps.

"And did you find anything after you've made such a mess?" He questioned.

"N-no. We didn't," I came back suddenly experiencing that uneasiness again. I nudged Becky in the ribs to start for the steps. She looked closely at my eyes for direction and understood that I wanted to get up to our rooms fast. I placed my hand on her back, trying to urge her to go faster. Looking back at me she noticed that I was trembling.

"I'll be happy to fix the hole Dad," I called down from the top of the steps. There was no response. In fact, I didn't even see Dad any longer. I guess he must have walked back to the other rooms, but why would he? It was so dark and he didn't have a flashlight. My fear did not subside as Becky and I raced up the double flight of stairs.

CHAPTER 9

" **W**hat's wrong?" Becky asked, totally out of breath as we climbed the second flight of steps to our rooms.

"Dad, he wasn't himself," I blurted out, "didn't you notice?"

"I guess so. I was so scared and I tried to hide this," she produced the brown box from under her buttoned up sweater.

"Whew, you're the best. I'm so glad you did that," I said, smiling at her. But then my smile quickly faded and I knew I had to get serious or Becky wouldn't listen to me, "I believe that William has control over Dad and sent him down to the basement to stop us, or at least to see if we found anything."

"You mean, like possession?" she asked.

"Yep. I hope it's just temporary. If not, we're

gonna get punished," I summed up with a serious nod of my head.

"Let's make sure the jewelry is really in here before we take it to Miss Summers," Becky suggested.

"Yeah and before Dad comes up here," I said.

We ran into my room and went inside the huge walk-in closet that Mom, Becky and I shared. I took down a big puzzle box from the top shelf and sat our find inside. With shaky hands I carefully opened it. Our mouths dropped in amazement as we gazed at a handful of beautiful jewelry. There were large, rounded diamond earrings, and an inch thick choker necklace of marquee cut diamonds. As we gently separated the tangled jewelry, we found a deep blue sapphire necklace, a bracelet of bright green emeralds mixed with diamond clusters and several rings that matched most of the necklaces.

"Wow," Becky whispered.

"Yeah, wow is right. This stuff really must be worth a fortune, let's put it all back and hide it in this puzzle box."

"We should take it to Miss Summers now," Becky urged.

"If the spirit of William is still in Dad then that's just what he'll expect us to do," I explained, trying my best to convince her. "Look, William doesn't want anyone else to have this, so he'll wait for us to take it to a living relative so he can find out who that person is and where they are. He just might get Dad to kill her," I said.

"He just might get Dad to kill us," she countered.

"Don't think I haven't thought of that too. Tonight we have to sleep light. Tomorrow, we'll sneak off and take this stuff to Miss Summers. Right now, let's start looking for that bottle."

With the jewelry safely stashed away we began our search in the three bedrooms that were used for storage. This was quick and easy because they all had adjoining doors. We opened all of them so we could keep an eye on each other while we searched. We moved boxes to the center of the rooms and got down on our hands and knees to look under the floorboard heaters. Then we stood on each other's shoulders and searched the narrow but long closets. Nothing. We did the same thing in all the rooms of the house. Still nothing.

We were in the stairwell looking for any weak spots in the wood when Mom passed by.

"What are you two doing?" she asked, looking at us like we were totally crazy.

"We're playing detective," Becky chimed in.

"Yeah, a murder has been committed and we have to find some clues," I added.

"Then I get to do the fingerprints," Becky smiled real big and produced a small pad of paper from her jeans pocket.

"All right, have fun," Mom said hesitantly, and went on her way - still giving us that look like she thought we were nuts.

"That was close," Becky whispered to me.

"Too close. Let's take a break and go back to my

room," I suggested.

The only bad thing about my room was that it didn't have a door. Someone could just walk right in at anytime. I stood guard at the doorway as Becky checked to make sure the jewelry was still in its hiding place. I pondered hiding it some place else, like in my cupboard. I had a little built-in cupboard in one corner of my room. It was really cool and I kept all kinds of stuff in it. Becky and I sat cross-legged on the floor at the foot of my bed and tried to think of where else we could look for that bottle. Suddenly, I felt a pressure against my back and jerked my head from side to side trying to see behind me.

"Melissa, what's wrong?" Becky asked.

"Josh," I whispered, "Josh, are you here?"

"Is he? Is he here?" Becky was getting excited.

"He's not saying anything, but it's the same feeling I get whenever he's close to me," I explained. We sat quietly for only a second until I heard a tiny clicking sound coming from my cupboard.

"Becky, look," I whispered, unable to move and staring at my cupboard door.

"No way," Becky's words came breathlessly.

The bottom door of the cupboard opened slowly with a quiet creak. We waited to see if something else would happen. When it didn't, I got up on all fours and slowly crawled over to the cupboard. I reached out with my hand to move some of my magazines out of the way when I suddenly felt

54

pressure on my wrist and a hard tug pulling me forward.

CHAPTER 10

" *T*his is it," I said, suddenly out of breath. "This is where we haven't looked yet."

"Hurry. Hand me some of that stuff," Becky was on her knees as I passed books, records, magazines and other teenage junk to her until the bottom of the cupboard was bare. I poked around the inner walls and found that there was a loose floorboard.

"Bingo!"

"Here, I'll go get the flashlight," Becky volunteered.

A few minutes later we had pried up the lose board and changed positions. I held the flashlight while Becky stuck her petite hands into the opening.

"Feel anything yet?" I asked.

"I'm trying, no, no wait...I got something," she said, grunting as she scraped her wrist while pulling out the prize. Without a word the two of us ran into the bathroom, quickly closing and locking the door.

Becky washed the bottle, rubbing it hard to get the ancient gook off. It was a tiny bottle only two inches tall, made of thick cut glass stained a light purple. It had a tiny stopper of cork that was sealed with a hard waxy substance. She held it up to the light and shook it slightly.

"I see it, the liquid is still in there," I announced.

"I don't believe it. We're actually gonna pull this thing off," Becky replied triumphantly.

The sudden pounding from upstairs chased away our happy mood in a split second. We looked up at the ceiling, which we thought would burst any moment; the stomping was really loud and very violent.

We ran out of the bathroom and back into my room. I took the bottle from Becky and put it in my jeans pocket.

"This must be the right bottle or he wouldn't be acting up," I commented.

Becky was so frightened that all she could do was just shake her head in agreement. Then we heard crashing sounds like furniture being broken, but to our knowledge there wasn't any furniture in the attic. It sounded like a herd of elephants had been turned loose up there, complete with a vibration that shook through the walls of the second floor.

"What are we going to do?" Becky blurted her words out so fast they seemed to run together. I just looked at her in total disbelief with no idea what to do.

"Becky! Melissa! Come down and eat!" Mom called up to us.

"Not now," I whined under my breath, "how are we going to eat with all this going on?"

"They can't hear it?" Becky asked following me out into the hall, while continuously looking up at the ceiling. "I can't believe they can't hear this noise."

"Told ya. Come on, we have to eat dinner, this is one thing we can't get out of."

Becky followed me down to the kitchen. Mom had a great meal on the table. She and Dad were happy and talking about all kinds of things during dinner and I was surprised that Dad didn't bring up the subject about the basement. We tried our best to join the conversation but it was hard to ignore the constant commotion going on up in the attic. I was very glad Dad was his old self again and that meant that William couldn't occupy two spaces at one time. As long as he kept making noise in the attic I felt safe and knew Becky and I didn't have to worry about Dad coming after us with William as his guide.

Later that night the sounds in the attic raged on. Not liking the sounds of violence, Becky climbed into my big full sized bed and lay close to me. She was very scared.

"Well, one thing for sure, we don't have to worry about sleeping." she tried to joke.

"Don't worry. I put the puzzle box under my

mattress and tied the bottle around my neck like a necklace, see," I dangled it in front of her face so she could see it in the dark. "Tomorrow, we'll take this stuff to school. We'll get a grownup involved - one that we can trust, and get them to call the police. On our lunch break I'll run over to my Uncle Steve's pharmacy and have him analyze this liquid. Hopefully, if it all comes together at one time, we'll then get the press involved," I took a deep breath as I realized there was a slight pause from the noise in the attic.

"We should get a police escort to Miss Summers' house and the press can take pictures of us handing over the jewelry to her," Becky put in.

"We'll tell them the whole story and then they can interview Uncle Steve. That will confirm everything and all the spirits will be at peace," I summed up with a smile.

The brief silence was broken as the walking in the attic began again; with hard, loud, determined steps. I assumed that William must've been listening to what we were saying. Now he knew his end would be coming soon.

CHAPTER 11

" *G*irls! Come on, get up!" Mom's voice brought Becky and I back to life from a restless night of hardly any sleep. I rolled onto my side and quickly fell on the floor with a loud thump.

"I can't believe we actually got some sleep," I grumbled from the floor as a pile of blankets fell on top of me.

"It's too early," Becky yawned and stretched and finished pushing the last of the blankets off the bed and on top of me.

"Let's get moving. I want to put an end to all this noise once and for all," I said.

"Boy, I agree with that. I don't want another night like last night."

Becky won first use of the bathroom. I made my bed, while waiting for my turn. I spread the sheets out and smoothed them down, I liked them neat and tight, and then I noticed a sunken spot in the center of the bed. I just stared at it for a second then tugged at the sheets a little to make them smooth again. It didn't budge. I walked closer to the side of the bed and waved my hands in the air above the depression. I didn't feel anything.

"Josh?" I questioned in a whisper.

"You two really have William upset," Josh answered.

I breathed a sigh of relief at hearing his voice and smiled. "Josh, I'm trying to make the bed. Do you mind?" I asked, gesturing toward the blankets. The spot on the bed disappeared. "It's good to hear you again. I hope you realize the kind of risks we're taking for you. We could get in all kinds of trouble," I told him.

"I know. I really do appreciate it. You just don't know what it's like to never rest, always wandering around the same place, and always thinking," he admitted.

"Doesn't sound like fun," I said.

"Melissa, no matter what happens, I want you to know that I think you're the best. I hope everything goes the way you've planned today. If it does you won't be hearing from me anymore," Josh said.

His words were positive, yet he sounded regretful and as he said them I could almost picture him smiling in a bashful kind of way.

"Thanks. Don't worry about us. I hate to say this but, I hope I don't hear from you anymore…" I said with a little giggle, "everyone should have

61

peace. By the way, will all this also get rid of William?"

"It should," Josh said.

"You mean you don't know?" I asked a bit annoyed.

"Well, I guess it will, I mean, I'm not really sure," Josh stammered.

"What!" I exclaimed.

"Don't worry Melissa. You're smart. If some type of surprise comes up I know you can handle it. I have lots of faith in you. Besides, I will try to help," he came back quickly.

"How?" I asked.

"I'll be watching and try to send you some helpful hints," he said.

"Any help you can give us would be great," I said.

The bathroom door opened and I could hear Becky going into her room.

"See ya," Josh said, quickly.

The day went as planned. On my lunch break I was able to go to my uncle's pharmacy. It was only a block away from the school and I noticed that a lot of kids who lived in town and close to school went home for lunch. So, I wasn't missed.

"Hi, Uncle Steve," I said, flinging the front door open and letting it bang shut as a little bell rang above it.

"Hey, Melissa. My how you're growing! What brings you here? I haven't seen you for a couple of months," he blurted out with a big smile. He greeted me with a bear hug and led me behind the counter with his arm still around me. I sat on a stool as he handed me an already made up deli sandwich and a soda from the stand-up cooler.

"Wow, thanks Uncle Steve. It's good to see you, too. I'd like to say that this is just a social call, but I have something very important to tell you. You're the only grownup I can confide in." I paused to take a bite out of my sandwich and a swallow of soda.

Uncle Steve stood back and looked at me solemnly with his arms crossed over his chest and fingers thoughtfully stroking his mustache. I assumed that Uncle Steve thought that something had gone wrong in my Mom's second marriage and was preparing himself for the worst. After several moments and another bite of my sandwich, he let out a deep breath and gave me his undivided attention.

"Okay, tell me what has happened," he finally said.

I produced the bottle from around my neck and sat it on the counter.

"This has happened," I began, "as well as a lot more weird stuff. Let me start at the beginning."

"At this point I think that would be best," he joked, happy that my problem wasn't what he thought it was. He put up his "Out To Lunch" sign, locked the front door, grabbed a sandwich too and sat down next to me. That was my cue to begin and I didn't spare him any details.

CHAPTER 12

I made it back to school just as the bell rang, which barely gave me enough time to make it to my next class. I had to decide which person to talk to about the jewelry and the history of the house. It had to be someone who was really cool and laid back...someone who understood about spirits and stuff like that...someone, hmmm, let's see. And then she passed me in the hall - my art teacher Mrs. Moore.

In between the sixth and seventh period classes, all the eighth graders got a twenty-minute break to go to the library, study, or prepare for the last class of the day. I took this time to go see Mrs. Moore.

All the kids liked Mrs. Moore. She was young, almost like a modern-day hippie and very understanding with all of us. She was so easy to trust, too. I found her sitting at her desk looking over artwork. She looked up and smiled at me when I walked in.

"Hey, Melissa," she said in a soft, soothing voice, "How's my star artist doing?"

"Fine," I replied, turning pink in the cheeks.

"I just finished going over some of your work. I must say, you really have potential girl!" she smiled lightly and her eyes twinkled with pride.

"Mrs. Moore, I have a problem and I feel you're the only one I can tell," I said breathlessly, letting the words fall out non-stop. "I really need your help."

"Well, did you talk to your parents first?" She asked.

"I did, but they don't believe me," I struggled with my words, "They can't hear the things I hear and they just laugh at me." That got her attention. She put the artwork aside and looked me straight in the eye.

"What are you saying?" She asked seriously.

"I've been hearing walking sounds in my attic, but it's worse than that. I also hear a voice talking to me. My sister and I did some research on the house we live in and discovered a terrible thing happened there long ago. We followed some leads and we discovered several things within the house to prove our theory, and now we need help to bring the truth out publicly." I said the words so fast I hardly took a breath, then flopped down on a stool close to Mrs. Moore.

Her elbows were on the counter, fingers laced

together and a hard look of concentration flashed across her face. After a few seconds of silence she finally spoke up.

"I'm sorry, I don't quite understand. You're talking in code. What kind of *things* have you discovered?" she asked.

I reached into my book bag and pulled out some of the jewelry. Her face went pale and her mouth hung open.

"Where did you get that?" She whispered.

"I told you. We found it in the house."

"Does this belong to your mother and you have a problem with stealing?"

"What? No! You're not paying attention to me. This jewelry belongs to a relative of the people who used to own our house. I want to get it back to her. I know who she is and where she is. Look, just let me tell you the whole story," I pleaded.

"All right, but it'd better be good," She looked into my eyes and I knew she would listen intently until I had finished my story. The twenty minutes were just about up, so I broke my story down and didn't go into a lot of details.

"Will you help me?" I asked once I had finished talking.

"I'm going to have to think on this one, kiddo," She said standing up and walking me to the door.

"But the spirits won't be at rest if we don't finish this today. I won't be at rest. No one will get any rest!" I pleaded.

"I need some time to make a few phone calls and

see what I can possibly do," She said with a reassuring smile.

The bell rang and the hall quickly filled with kids going to their last class. I felt so depressed and helpless as I filtered in with the crowd. Uncle Steve would have the results of the testing tomorrow. Maybe Mrs. Moore would actually help me, maybe not. My faith in her had suddenly diminished. She's hesitating, has to *think* on it and make a few phone calls. Geez! I need action *now* and no one is willing to jump right away and ask questions later. Well, all right, maybe *I* could make a phone call or two myself.

CHAPTER 13

*B*ecky and I got home before our parents did and that gave us some time to devise the next step to our plan. We quickly hid the jewelry, got a snack, and sat at the kitchen table with the phone book.

"Who are you going to call first?" Becky asked, sitting on her knees in the chair and leaning close.

"The local newspaper. Maybe I can sucker a starving reporter into coming out here," I said, "I know I've altered our original plans but things are working out anyway."

I quickly dialed the number and it didn't take long to get someone on the phone that was willing to listen to my story.

"Now, where did you say you lived?" The young man named Jason asked again.

"Twenty seven Wakefield Road," I answered.

"This is just such an incredible story..." he began, but I quickly cut him off.

"Yes, I know but you have to believe me. No one else will. No one will help me prove it's all true. Just think of the reviews you'll get!" I tried my best to con him. He was very gullible it seemed, for a reporter.

"W-well, I guess you're right..." he stumbled on his words.

"Please say you'll come out here tomorrow around six. I should have all the proof you'll need. Then we'll take the jewelry to the oldest living relative and present it to her. I'll show you I'm telling the truth and that this is not some childish prank!" I pleaded.

"Well, okay, I'll be there," Jason agreed.

"You know how to get here?" I asked.

"Yes. Your house is so big I can see it from the main road," Jason said.

"Thank you so very much. Good-bye." I hung up the phone and smiled at Becky. We were so excited that we actually got someone to listen and believe us that we grabbed each other's hands and jumped up and down. The feeling of triumph overwhelmed me and I soon forgot about the danger that lurked within our house. That's when I suddenly noticed Becky had stopped jumping with me and fear coursed icily through my veins when I saw the expression on her face. She stared at something over my shoulder.

"What? What is it?" I asked in a very small

voice, ceasing my jumping and becoming too afraid to move.

Her expression had turned to one of horror as she continued to stare. I jerked my head around in the direction of her gaze just in time to see the basement door opening on its own.

"Don't get upset. Mom always latches the top latch. Maybe she just forgot this time and a breeze through the house is pulling the door open," I said convincingly. But who was I trying to convince - me or Becky? As I talked I gathered my nerve and slowly approached the basement door. Becky was right behind me, practically stepping on my heels and hanging onto my arm. Once I got close enough, I tried to see around the corner of the doorjamb and down the basement steps. I didn't want to get too close. What if something was right there, just inside, waiting to grab me?

I felt myself shake with every step I took. Then I started to put out my hand so I could shut the door - reaching with trembling fingers and waiting for a huge hairy paw to grab me! My mind flashed back to the sniffing noise at the attic door. What if that thing was here now and I was so very close? All it had to do was reach out and I would be a goner!

Suddenly, we heard all the doors upstairs open with a loud and echoing click and it made us automatically look toward the stairway. I started wondering if something would come down to get us or jump out of the basement instead. Just at that moment Becky started to whimper and hold her stomach, due to the fact that she always gets sick when she's really scared. Then in a whirlwind of confusion all the doors slammed shut at the same time and that also included the basement door. Seizing the opportunity, I lunged forward pressing my weight against the door and fumbled with the top latch, but I just couldn't seem to get the latch into the lock!

The doors upstairs opened again. This time they opened and shut very quickly and repeatedly. Over and over they opened and shut. The noise was so loud and violent I thought they would all be in pieces very soon. We had to get upstairs and stop all this craziness before Becky and I were blamed for any damages.

After straining and fumbling with the latch I just barely got it onto the hook when a sudden weight from behind the door knocked me backwards. The latch was just barely on the hook, but it was holding and the door shuddered as the weight bumped it repeatedly. Becky finally snapped out of her terrified state and leaped forward. She threw her body against the barrier and pushed the latch all the way onto the hook, then stepped back. The angry *something* behind the door continuously bumped against it, making the basement door vibrate. Becky maneuvered to my side and glanced at me with a newly acquired look of triumph and bravery.

"That was great!" I yelled over the noise of the slamming doors, praising her for her actions.

"Should we go up?" she asked.

"We have to. If anything is damaged, who do you think will get in trouble?" I replied, pressing my lips together and shaking off any fear. In a very determined manner I ran up the stairs to the second floor with Becky close on my heels.

Once we appeared at the top of the steps the doors slammed shut once more and stayed that way. We stood in the hallway waiting for the echo to settle.

"Give it up William!" I finally shouted into the air, "Your spirit will finally rest whether you like it or not!"

There was silence and then a deep, echoing laugh. Ice water ran through my veins and a shiver spidered up my spine as I listened. Becky and I glanced at each other, her eyes were filled with terror and it was at that moment when I suddenly lost my courage. Then just as suddenly as it began the laugh faded into the walls and all was quiet

CHAPTER 14

*J*ust as I finished my statement to William, Mom walked in the front door. "Becky, Melissa!" she exclaimed, "Why aren't you two doing your homework?"

Our shoulders slumped forward at the same time and we let out a disgruntled sigh. I scrunched up my face. Becky did the same.

"We'll be right down Mom," I called.

"You know she's going to want to know what we've been doing all this time since we haven't been doing our homework at the kitchen table," Becky warned.

"I know. That's okay though," I came back with a wry smile, "I've been doing research on a paper before I actually started to write it - how about you?"

Catching the gist of where I was coming from,

Becky quickly formulated an excuse of her own. "I did most of mine on the bus on the way home," she said, with an imitation of my smile.

"Let's not make lying a habit though, okay?" I added as we turned to go downstairs. Becky shook her head in agreement because we both knew we'd have to find time to secretly do our real homework and not let Mom catch us, besides getting caught in a lie was the absolute worst thing.

Bedtime came way too fast. I was a little worried that it was going to be another restless night but William had been quiet all evening after the earlier door incident.

I felt I had to tell Mom what had been going on and what Becky and I had been up to. She should also be aware of the reporter coming to visit at six o'clock tomorrow and why. I had to be tactful and hopefully catch her in a good mood.

Becky had gone to her room to read and Mom was in the living room filing her nails.

"Mom, can we talk?" I approached her, wringing my hands, while sitting next to her on the sofa.

"Sure. What's up?" she said happily.

"Remember when Becky and I went to visit the old people who live close by?" I began.

"Yeah…" she said.

"We found out that the lady who lives two houses over is an actual living relative of the people who used to own this house," I stated carefully.

"Really?" she asked.

"Her name is Miss Summers and she's really

nice. She told us a story about a tragic thing that happened to the people who used to live in this house," I said.

"Really? What happened?" she stopped filing her nails and turned her undivided attention to me.

I told her the whole story about Josh and William, the jewelry and the poison. She listened closely and didn't move a muscle, but I did notice her jaw muscles getting tight. I had hoped she actually believed me this time.

"Becky and I decided it would be cool to see if anything she told us was true. So we searched the house and found the jewelry and the bottle with the liquid in it," I was saying when she suddenly drew herself up and blinked.

"You what?" she asked in total disbelief.

"I took the bottle to Uncle Steve and he'll have the results tomorrow. If there was really any poison in that tea, he should be able to find out what kind," I blurted out.

"I can't believe you did that!" her voice started getting louder with every word, "And not telling me any of this? Well, it's almost the same as lying!"

"I tried to tell you but you wouldn't believe me!" I shouted back.

"Melissa, I swear, what is the matter with you? What would possess you to do all this?"

"All the weird stuff that's happening in this house that's what!"

"I don't hear or see anything weird going on."

"That's the point! Only kids can hear it. You've

stood right next to me while the noise was going on and you still didn't hear it. Now please calm down and stop yelling at me."

She took a deep breath and cleared her throat. I could see her hands shaking from rage as she reached for the arm of the sofa to steady herself and scoot back on the cushion. Once her fury began to fade I decided to continue.

"The jewelry is safe, too. I hid it in my locker at school until I get the results about the poison." This time I did lie, but only because she had me so nervous that I suddenly didn't trust her. If I had told her where the jewelry *really* was, she might have taken it away and ruined my plans.

"That was really very smart of you to do that," she said in a calmer voice. "So what's you're next move since you've already gone this far?"

"Once I get the test results back, and if it's positive, I have invited a reporter to come here at six o'clock tomorrow so I can prove everything is true. Then we're going over to Miss Summers' house and present her with the lost family fortune," I said with a smile.

"Melissa! I can't believe you went so far with this," she scolded.

"Mom, look, it's the only way. What else was I to do? Wouldn't you like some help if you were a lost spirit?" I countered.

"Yes, but…" This time I cut her off.

"Come on Mom. I've confided in you. I've told you everything because I really need your support.

Isn't that what mothers and daughters are suppose to do?" I pleaded giving her a pitiful look and batting my lashes at her. She looked disgusted and upset but ready to surrender. She was quiet for a minute or two, most likely trying to sort out her thoughts, then took a deep breath.

"Well, all right." She gave in with a defeated sigh and I broke out in a big smile, "You've already done all this other stuff. What else am I to do? Even if there is no poison in the bottle you must give that jewelry to Miss Summers tomorrow. Someone may try to say you stole it and then you'll be in real trouble. I don't know anything about noises in this house. I have never heard anything."

"That's because you're a grownup," I cut in.

"I don't want to hear that silly stuff. I'm only going to let you do this because after tomorrow I don't want to hear another word about it. If it all falls through and you're embarrassed then you will have to deal with it. If only half of it works out then you'll get the satisfaction of returning the jewelry." She turned away from me suddenly and started filing her nails again.

"Thanks Mom, you're the best," I said, hugging her.

"Melissa, I mean it. I don't want to hear any more about noises in this house or any strange happenings," she said sternly, shaking the nail file at me. "I want you girls to concentrate on your schoolwork. Don't waste your time playing Dick Tracy, or Agatha Christie, or whoever, okay?"

"Sure, you got it," I agreed. I kissed her good night and went upstairs to fill Becky in on my conversation with Mom.

CHAPTER 15

*B*ecky was relieved after I told her the results of my conversation with Mom, but then gave me a worried look.

"What is it?" I asked.

"Well, Miss Summers will have the family fortune back, Josh's spirit will be at peace, but will it all make William's spirit go away?" she wondered out loud.

"Even Josh couldn't tell me that one for sure," I said, getting up from the edge of her bed and walking into my room. "I guess we'll just have to play it by ear and hope for the best."

Becky turned off her light and snuggled under her blankets. "It's freezing in here," she commented.

"It sure is. It's cold outside," I agreed, hugging myself for warmth.

"William really bothers me Melissa," Becky said

quietly with a yawn, "If this doesn't work and he won't go away, I just might ask to go live with my Mom."

I felt a big empty spot in the pit of my stomach when she said that. I didn't want her to go, not after all we had been through. She did get on my nerves but lately I've really loved having her around. She was the only one who believed me right from the start. She backed me up and helped me every step of the way. My mouth went dry as I searched for the right words to say.

"Don't worry Becky, everything will work out. Trust me." Becky leaving was all I could think of as I got into bed and turned off the light.

Even though it was quiet for a change I still couldn't sleep. I kept waking up, tossing and turning. It was very cold in the house - colder than normal. I thought I could hear Becky moving around in her bed and I wondered if she was awake.

I sat up in bed, letting my eyes adjust to the darkness and looked through the doorway into Becky's room. I couldn't see her but I did see the curtains in her room blowing around.

"That's why it's so cold," I said quietly. I got out of bed and went into Becky's room. "Becky, did you know your window was open all this time?" As I asked the question I pulled back the curtain and discovered that the window was already closed. "Hey, guess what?" I walked over to her bed to shake her and she wasn't there.

"Becky, where are you?"

I walked out into the hall and looked in the bathroom. She wasn't in there. Maybe she went downstairs? I could hear the TV on in the living room and Mom snoring. Wow, she must really be tired to snore like that!

"Becky!" I called again then strained my ears to pick up any sounds - and I did. A slight shuffling of feet was coming from the end of the hallway down by the attic. I slowly walked down the hall and heard a muffled sound, one that I had heard before and could never forget. It started off soft and became progressively louder with every step that I took. My heart began pounding uncontrollably and my breath quickened as I came closer to the sound. Something wasn't right, I could feel it. As I rounded the corner, I beheld a sight that made my blood freeze in my veins.

CHAPTER 16

*B*ecky was standing with her hand extended toward the latch to the attic door and the sniffing sound from around the edges heightened with excitement. Scratching and clawing replaced the sniffing and the bottom right hand corner of the attic door shuddered under the unseen force. The thing wanted out again and it was trying to use Becky to do it!

Becky looked like she was sleepwalking and her movements were awkward and unsure. I was mesmerized by the entire scene - totally transfixed in my spot. It felt like something was keeping me from moving and keeping me from stopping Becky. My mind knew I had to move…to stop her…to stop this whole crazy thing from happening! But my body wouldn't respond; for the moment I could only watch.

Then the door began to bend in and out from the weight of the creature. The wood creaked and the hinges groaned under the pressure. It was so cold I could see my breath, and as I stood there with my mouth hanging open it seemed as if time had stopped. Even though everything that was happening took only a few minutes, time seemed to drag, as though everything was traveling in slow motion.

Finally Becky began to move forward again and the sounds behind the attic door stopped. She took one step forward and placed her hand on the latch then paused for a brief moment. It was just at that moment I regained control of myself.

"No!" I shouted. I quickly moved forward, knocking her hand away from the latch and pushing her against the door to Mom's room. Holding her by the shoulders, I looked into her stunned face and she finally blinked her eyes.

"Melissa, what happened?"

"Didn't you realize what you were doing?" I asked.

"Why did you trick me into coming down here?" she asked, frightened and angry. She pushed back her long blonde hair and put her hands on her hips.

"It wasn't me!" I argued looking surprised and a bit hurt. "It was William. He wants you to let him out of the attic so he can stop us."

"You expect me to believe that?" she came back, now angry at me and, I guessed, thinking I was lying to her.

"Look, think a minute. We've been avoiding this spot for days. It's freezing in here, no windows are open, and I just saw your curtains blowing by themselves. Remember all the stuff we've read about? Well, this is one of those things an angry spirit does," I said.

"You're right," Becky admitted after a brief pause. "Environmental control is one of the things evil spirits like to do, as well as making things levitating or trying to use dreams to manipulate people. I remember that from one of those books."

"Yeah, you're back to normal," I said with a smile.

Suddenly, the sniffing at the door started up again, this time it was accompanied by a low, rumbling growl. It sounded almost like the growl of a lion. We stared at the door as we slowly inched our way past it huddled together.

"Hurry!" Becky whispered, more to herself than to me.

Then there was a pounding - like the pounding of a fist or more like something throwing it's whole body against the door. It pounded three times and then paused. Then it pounded three more times and paused. I noticed that the latch wasn't locked all the way anymore. When I knocked Becky's hand away from the latch earlier she had moved it slightly up. It was nearly unlocked! Now as the vibration from the pounding continued, the latch was steadily moving upwards.

Just as I sprang forward to push the latch back

down again the door flew open. I was knocked backwards into Becky by a tremendous gust of wind. It was raging and powerful - so powerful that I could hardly move. I struggled to open my eyes and look at the open doorway for I wanted to see what it was.

In the wind I saw a white cloud billowing around the opening of the doorway. It stayed in one place like a swirling cloud mixed with open air, rolling and twisting in space. Roiling, cold air rolled down the last two steps of the attic stairway. It reminded me of how the mist tumbles out of a huge freezer when the door is left open.

Somehow I managed to slowly stand up, I was ready to face the spirit completely unafraid. This was it - our confrontation - the dreaded moment. I had to do whatever it took to get rid of this thing once and for all, but what? Standing in front of the swirling cloud and fighting to stay upright made me feel weak. Maybe that's what it's trying to do? Wear me down and make me feel defeated? I wondered if it knew how I was feeling right now?

I glanced behind me to see Becky cowering in the corner in a sitting position with her arms covering her head. I couldn't let anything happen to her; I was the oldest. Besides, it was my fault all this was happening and I had dragged her into it. I had to be the one to make all this stop. I swallowed any doubt and did my best to clear my mind of any fear. I stepped closer to the door holding myself steady and prepared myself for the worst.

"You're a big loser, William!" I shouted above all the wind. "Take all your silly magic tricks and go back to where ever you came from. I order you to go back! I order you to go back! You're not welcome here!"

I had no idea if anything I was saying would have any effect on the situation. I'd seen so many scary movies where the good guy fought ghosts, spirits or poltergeist with words, Biblical phrases or did something very tricky. Not being very good at thinking on my feet, I had nothing in mind at the time. Yet, I continued to stand before the swirling cloud, refusing to give up, until I realized something was beginning to take shape within the center of the white mass. The image took my breath away and made me take several steps back.

CHAPTER 17

*T*hrough the swirling cloud the shape of a hideous skull came into view. It scowled at me and its mouth was twisted into an evil grin. It started growing and filling the whole doorway. I just stood there and stared. I felt so helpless and small. What was I going to do?

I allowed my eyes to glance around. There wasn't anything close by that I could use to defend myself. This thing was totally evil and I had to think fast! Then I remembered Sunday school classes when I was little and got an idea. I started to recite the twenty-third Psalm. I repeated it out loud...over and over, while staring back at the skull and challenging it to stop me.

I realized as I spoke that the cold air was suddenly receding. The skull began howling and screeching as if in pain, its image wavering, then fading. The wailing made my skin crawl but I didn't stop.

Out of the corner of my eye I noticed a slight movement of the door and the latch. The door was being pushed shut slowly yet steadily by invisible hands. Josh! I kept repeating the twenty-third Psalm over and over as the door inched closed more and more, then ended my recital just when it closed completely and the latched flipped over into the locked position again.

"Josh, I'm so glad you're here!" I said with a big sigh of relief.

"That was quick thinking Melissa but you've only weakened him for the moment," Josh informed me.

"Thanks. I just didn't know what else to do," I said raising my hands at my side in a gesture of surrender.

But I cut the conversation short and turned my attention to Becky who was still on the floor, slumped in an unmoving heap.

"Becky! Becky!" I said shaking her. "I think she passed out."

"She'll be okay. Listen, you've got to seal this door a little more. William will be back and he'll be really mad," Josh warned.

"What in the world was all that?" Becky asked in a groggy voice. I helped her get up and held onto her arm until she could stand on her own.

"That was William trying his best to enter our time and space," I replied. "Thanks to Josh,

William is closed up in the attic again. Do you feel okay?" Becky nodded her head affirmatively. "Good. Listen, go down stairs and get Dad's hammer and a couple of those two-inch nails real fast."

Becky quickly regained her composure and ran down the steps without questioning me.

"Josh, you still here?" I asked, once she had left.

"I'm right here Melissa," he said.

"Tomorrow will bring an end to many things. The jewelry will be given to its rightful owner and that story will be printed in the paper for everyone to read," I stated, but stopped talking at the sound of Becky running back upstairs with the hammer and nails.

"I'll do it," she proclaimed, clutching the hammer so I wouldn't take it away. I let her hammer the nails around the door, making sure they were bent inward so the door could not be opened without twisting them out of the way. When she was finished Becky went back downstairs to put the hammer away.

Once she was gone again, I continued to talk to Josh as I walked back to my room. "If poison is found in the bottle, then the truth about you will also be published and you will finally be at peace."

"Wow, I can't believe it's finally gonna happen for me, after all this time," Josh said happily.

"I have to figure out what it will take to get rid of William," I said, coming to a stop by Becky's doorway and folding my arms over my chest, while

89

releasing a deep sigh. Just then Becky came running back upstairs.

"Mom just woke up and she's turning off the lights," she reported.

"I know this whole thing tonight is the straw that broke the camel's back," I began as I looked pleadingly into Becky's face, "but just wait until everything is out in the open tomorrow before you make any hasty decisions, okay?"

"This will be my last week here if this doesn't work. I refuse to live in a house where creepy stuff is constantly happening. Deal?" She held up a crooked pinky, looking me in the eye.

"Deal!" I came back with a smile and laced my pinky in hers in the form of a pinky swear.

We heard Mom's heavy footsteps coming up the stairs and we bolted to our beds, trying our best to pretend to be asleep. Mom had no idea what had just happened and I blamed that on William putting her under another deep sleeping spell. I mean, what else could it be? Ever since the walking in the attic began she's been falling asleep on the sofa. She falls into such a deep sleep and she doesn't hear anything that's going on upstairs.

This time it was for the best, however. I had already gotten an agreement out of Mom about tomorrow and I wasn't going to bring anything else up. I knew it just might push her past the limits of her patience.

CHAPTER 18

*D*uring my school lunch break the next day, I ran over to Uncle Steve's pharmacy. I was totally out of breath as I pushed open the front door and headed for the counter. Uncle Steve was waiting for me with a big smile on his face.

"I was wondering when you would get here," he teased.

"So, what did you find out?" I asked, feeling butterflies in my stomach while I waited for him to answer.

"I'm really very proud of you kiddo," he said. He handed me a copy of the test results. Even though I looked at it and listened to him, I didn't understand anything on that paper. "There really was poison in that bottle mixed with some tea. It took a lot of analyzing because it was so old but it really was there!"

"Can I have that statement in writing and with your signature on it?" I asked.

"Sure. Just hold on one minute and I'll prepare something real official-looking," he said, walking back to his desk.

For the rest of the day I was feeling nervous and yet relieved. I had the jewelry in my book bag along with the report about the poison. I was all set to do what had to be done. I would finally solve an age-old mystery and everyone would be at peace, everyone except William. What was I going to do? Not only was his spirit frightening, he was becoming bolder and more threatening every time he made his presence known. I was in deep thought when a hand came up from behind, touched me on the shoulder and startled me so badly that I spun around to see who it was.

Mrs. Moore was standing there with a lovely smile on her kind face. Her long, curly hair was hanging down loosely and she was wearing an excessive amount of jewelry today, which made her look very much like a hippie.

"Hey Melissa," she said quietly.

"Hey Mrs. Moore," I replied.

"I've thought a lot about our conversation from the other day and I think I may have a solution to your spirit problem," she said.

"Really! That's great! Can I come see you during my free time?"

"That'll be fine," she said.

During my twenty-minute break I raced to Mrs.

Moore's classroom. When I entered her room she was going through a book on myths and ghosts. She looked up and smiled at me and motioned for me to sit next to her.

"Okay, I'll try to explain this the best I can. You have to really understand what you're getting yourself into and there can be no mistakes," she said in one long breath.

"You're making me feel like I want to just move away and let someone else deal with this," I said somewhat reserved.

"It's too late for that. You've gone too far to stop now," she said in a gentle voice, placing her hand on top of mine to reassure me. I shook my head in agreement and swallowed hard. I stared into her eyes as she unveiled a mythical secret I had never heard of before.

"This apparition is more than just a poltergeist, it's a severely disturbed and very angry spirit. There are no acts of exorcism to get rid of it. Reciting the Biblical word can only weaken it. Therefore, you must trap this spirit inside an object from which it cannot escape."

She held out a tiny pyramid-shaped crystal. It gave off sparkles of light as she held it in the palm of her hand and moved it slightly. The sight of it dazzled my eyes. I reached out to touch it but she daintily withdrew the crystal pyramid and set it out of my reach.

"A crystal is only powerful after it is given to a person as a gift," she explained. "It becomes even

93

more powerful if that person is a friend. Crystals have been used over the centuries in rituals and as charms. Their power is unlimited. Crystals also refract light and defuse it."

"So, what does this have to do with my spirit problem?" I asked.

"You will trap your spirit in this and then bury it deep in the ground," she finished.

"You're kidding right?" I asked. "How am I supposed to do that?"

"You must place the crystal in front of a window where the light comes in strong. At the precise moment that the sun strikes it, you must lure the spirit toward it. When he is encased or encircled by the light from the crystal he will be blinded. When the spirit tries to retreat he will be confused. All he will see is the dark spot at the bottom of the crystal where the light begins. This is the entrance to the crystal. The spirit will then flee into the darkness and find himself trapped within a world of bright light," she explained.

"Mrs. Moore, the chance of me getting that to happen is one in a million," I began.

"You can do it Melissa. You're creative and you don't give up."

"What if this doesn't work?" I whined.

"It will. Just remember one thing. Once the spirit is in the crystal remove it from the light immediately or the spirit will escape."

I sighed a deep, troubled sigh and looked into her blue eyes. She looked so confident. She really wanted me to do this. "Okay," I finally agreed in a defeated manner.

With a big smile, she reached for the crystal pyramid and presented it to me. "Here is a beautiful gift for you my friend. Use it wisely." She pressed it into my hands. I gingerly took it from her, cupped the crystal in my palms and held it close to my heart.

"I will. Thank you Mrs. Moore," I said with a serious smile and a short nod of my head.

"Good luck," she said.

I thought to myself, as I left her room, "this is a three-sided figure. A triangle, a pyramid and it reminded me of...oh my, my house! Of course, that's why William was stuck in the attic. The roof over each of the three windows in the attic was in the shape of a triangle; three windows on three sides of the house. I never thought of that before! And that's why William could only come out if he was invited."

Now I was armed with a new type of knowledge and my courage began to build deep inside my gut.

CHAPTER 19

"*M*elissa, I don't want to do this," Becky whined as she struggled to keep up with me. We covered the driveway with long, hurried strides as I tried my best to ignore her whining and keep my mind on exactly what I was supposed to do with the crystal.

"We have to do this right now, Becky. The sun goes down early in the winter and Mom will be home in two hours. Once William is gone, we can wait for the reporter and do the rest of the things we need to do without worrying." I paused outside our house and took a deep breath, while looking into Becky's face. "Look, stop worrying. Stay in the kitchen if that will make you feel better."

I opened the door and was in for a surprise. The whole house was in motion! The cupboard doors were opening and closing rapidly, accompanied by the sound of wind and low moaning. The only good thing was that there really wasn't any wind, just the sound. Pots and pans rattled on the shelves and the rug in front of the sink skittered around the floor. I was really getting tired of the floorshow and quickly went to work. I put my book bag on the kitchen table and grabbed a handful of the jewelry and the crystal. Then I handed my book bag to Becky.

"Hold on to this. The rest of the jewelry is in here. No matter what, don't let go of it!" I ordered.

"What are you going to do with that?" she asked, eyeing the treasure collected in my hand.

"Bait!" I replied with a wry smile.

I raced up the stairs and stopped at the entrance to the hallway. The corridor stretched out before me. Suddenly it looked so long and far away that I felt as though I would never reach the end. No, this wasn't happening. This was a trick, an illusion. He was not going to make me feel inferior. I squeezed my eyes shut and opened them again and the illusion was gone, the hallway was its usual length. But, how much time had lapsed? It felt as if I had stood there for hours but I couldn't be sure. The only thing I noticed was the sun beginning to go down and I could see it through the big window down at the end of the hall right outside the attic door.

I started walking with determined steps toward the attic. The doors to the unused bedrooms on my right were shaking and rattling. I could feel the vibrations from them deep in my gut but it only made me move faster.

Once at my destination, I laid the jewelry on the floor and placed the crystal on a cardboard box in front of it. Then I bent the nails away from the edges of the door. It was at that time I had noticed all the haunting sounds had stopped. The house was suddenly very quiet, but for only a few brief moments.

The silence was broken by the sound of walking in the attic. The walking sounds were strong, loud and very determined. They pounded their way down the steps and stopped behind the door.

I stared at the door, my breath quickening. I was ready. I glanced out the window. The sun was dipping down and it was shining brightly though the window. It was so bright that it was beginning to touch the crystal. I had to hurry.

"You win William," I shouted. "You can have the jewelry back. You're a selfish, evil child and you'll never be at peace." I paused when I heard three loud pounding sounds on the attic door. "Well, come on! You have to come and take it yourself."

I stepped back and pressed myself against the wall around the corner then slid my hand around and lifted the latch, but quickly withdrew it afterwards. The door was opened only a crack - nothing was holding it shut and nothing was happening.

A sudden gust of wind blew the door open and along with it came a vile stench. My hair whipped around my face as I held my position and peaked around the side of the wall. My eyes beheld a sight that made me want to vomit. A walking corpse was only an arm's length away. It was a boy, no older than myself, with tattered nineteenth century clothing and rotting flesh. His skin (what little he had) hung loosely from his bones. He was practically all bone. As he moved, his body made sickening squishy sounds. I clapped a hand over my mouth and tried not to scream. I had to stay focused on the plan. I watched the sun. It was moving faster now but would it be fast enough?

William was right in front of the crystal. He looked down at the harmless-looking crystal sitting on the small, empty box then he noticed the jewelry on the floor. He stepped over the crystal with a decaying leg and began to bend down to pick up the jewelry. I held my breath. The sun wasn't going to make it. I was doomed. How would I stop William now?

Just at that moment William paused. He sensed my presence and looked over at me then stared into my face and grinned a toothless smile; his eyes were barely in their sockets and I swore I could see maggots crawling all over his face. I felt my body go cold and my heart stop. What was he thinking? What was he going to do? My answer came quickly.

CHAPTER 20

*T*he corpse of William slowly stood up, forgetting about the jewelry and continuing to stare at me.

"You..." he said, in a hoarse and gravelly voice.

I felt my knees buckle and I couldn't move, I couldn't cry out for Becky and I refused to sink to the floor. I just leaned against the wall, totally terrified and shaking uncontrollably.

I forced my eyes away from the sight of William and looked out of the window at the sun. It dipped a little more and hit the crystal. A tremendous amount of light bounced off of the charmed object, shot in all directions and enveloped William's body.

He let out a loud, pained scream. The more the sun moved the brighter the light from the crystal became. It was so bright I couldn't see him anymore, but he was there, I could hear him howling and screaming.

I got down on my hands and knees and crawled over to the jewelry, grabbed it up and stuffed it in my shirt and pants pockets then I looked up at where William had been standing. I was so close that I could touch him but he wasn't there anymore. Well, he was, but he had reverted to his vaporous, insubstantial form again.

I stayed down low and watched the sun go behind the hills in the distance. As the horrible howling sound continued, William was suddenly sucked up into the crystal in one loud and sudden *swoop*! I quickly grabbed the crystal pyramid and nervously shoved it in a little black bag that I had stuffed in my jeans pocket. I was still shaking as I sat on the floor against the wall, trying my best to control my pounding heart and sporadic breathing. I wiped at the cold sweat that had formed on my brow.

"It's over!" I whispered out loud to myself, "Finally things will get back to normal." I stood up and closed the attic door. Just as a precaution, I turned a few nails back around to block the door from being opened from the inside. It just made me feel better to do that.

"Becky!" I shouted running down the stairs, "It's over! I got him! He's trapped forever."

Becky met me at the bottom of the steps. When she saw the overly excited and happy look on my face she gave me a big smile of relief. I stood in front of her and showed her the little black bag.

"He's in here, inside the crystal," I said gesturing to the bag as I held it up to her face. I opened it ever so slightly and allowed her to peak inside.

"Is he really in there?" she asked.

"Witnessed it with my own two eyes," I guaranteed. "But we can't take the crystal out of the darkness. As soon as light hits it, he will escape."

"Well, we can't have that, can we?" Becky replied.

Just at that moment we heard mom's car coming up the gravel driveway.

"Let's get things cleaned up fast," Becky ordered.

"I'll go get the brown case for the jewelry. You tidy up anything that was thrown out of place," I commanded.

CHAPTER 21

*A*fter Mom came home, Becky and I checked the rest of the house to see if anything else had been knocked out of place by the earlier commotion. Once our curiosity was satisfied we sat in the kitchen and waited for the reporter.

Six o'clock had come and gone. I was getting restless and upset. Why hadn't he come? He said he would. He even gave me his word, didn't he? I was really getting depressed. We had everything ready to show him; the bottle, the test results and the jewelry. Even Mom couldn't believe her eyes.

"This jewelry is absolutely beautiful," she said, lightly fingering the diamond choker. "I'm really proud of you two. I'm glad you let me in on your secret."

There was a knock at the door and it made all of us jump. Mom opened the door to reveal a fresh faced young man. He was tall with light brown hair and eyes and he wore glasses. He was slender in build and carried a camera and some recording equipment.

"Hi, I'm Jason Turner, from the local paper. Is there a Melissa here?" he asked in one breath.

I ran to the door and stood between Jason and my Mom with an extended hand.

"Hi, I'm Melissa," I said eagerly.

"Please come in Mr. Turner," Mom said. Jason came inside and took the whole kitchen in at a glance before he finally smiled at Becky and me and shook my hand.

"This is really a big place," he commented.

"Yep, it sure is," I said. "Are you ready to hear my story?" I knew I was appearing a bit anxious but I didn't care, I wanted to get the rest of my plan over and done with. I took Jason by his coat sleeve and led him to the kitchen table. He put down everything he was carrying and stopped short when his eyes caught sight of the jewelry.

"Wow, you weren't kidding," he said, looking at me and smiling. I just smiled back at him and blushed. I saw Becky rolling her eyes at me and scrunching up her nose. I just ignored her. This was my time to be in the spotlight and I was going to enjoy every minute of it.

"All right, Melissa, I'm all set. The recorder is on and you can begin your story. After you're finished we'll go visit Miss Summers and present her with the jewelry and I'll take a few pictures.

How does that sound?" Jason said.

"Sounds good," I said, "Okay, now here's what happened." I told him the whole story and didn't leave out any details. I explained everything, from the day we moved into the house right up to the part where I trapped William in the crystal. Of course Becky had to chime in her bits and pieces to add to the story. I guess that was fair, after all, she helped and backed me up along the way.

I showed him the bottle that had the poison in it and Uncle Steve's report. We showed him where we found it and elaborated on the more creepy details of what happened when we found it.

Of course he wanted to see the attic. I wasn't a bit afraid as I led him through the house with Mom and Becky tagging along. I opened the attic door and flipped on the light switch while everyone followed me up the stairs. The attic was barren and dusty. There was one huge open living space and two separate rooms on either side of it. I could almost picture Josh and the other servants living up here and what it must have looked like. Becky chattered endlessly to Jason as they looked around the big room. I had stopped and leaned against the doorjamb to one of the empty rooms, waiting for them to finish checking things out.

Suddenly a transparent looking figure caught my eye. I turned my head around and looked directly at it. There, in the center of the room where I was standing was a boy dressed in nineteenth century clothing. He was a little shorter than me with blonde hair. He was very slim and very cute. I caught my breath when he smiled at me and blew a kiss. I just stood there in amazement until he waved at me.

"Bye Melissa...and thank you," his voice lightly echoed in my head and a blanket of warmth suddenly enveloped me then, just as quickly, lifted.

"Bye Josh," I whispered to him and returned a sad, yet happy smile. I didn't take my eyes from him until he completely faded away.

I was jerked back into reality by the sound of voices from the others coming closer to me. Jason was anxious to see Miss Summers, give her the jewelry and finish his interviews.

We locked up the attic and hurried down to the kitchen. Becky carried the jewelry securely inside the brown case. I gave Jason the bottle with the poison still in it and a copy of the test results. He packed everything up and the four of us went to see Miss Summers.

Miss Summers was very happy to see Becky and me again. She invited all of us into her cozy little sitting room then took her place in her favorite chair. Everyone sat except me, as I recited the story once again. After I was finished, Jason readied his camera as Becky opened the old brown case with the jewelry in it and presented it to Miss Summers.

Poor Miss Summers looked as if she would have heart failure. Her eyes became huge and she gasped for air for a few seconds then she became very still and quiet. We stared at her to make sure she was all right until she suddenly came to life and began to cry. Tears of happiness streaked down her cheeks as she reached out and hugged Becky and me. Even my Mom was getting teary-eyed over the whole scene. Jason took a lot of pictures and then he decided it was time for us to go.

On the way back to our house, Jason asked to see the crystal. I reluctantly pulled the black bag out of my pocket.

"Well, how can I see it if you don't take it out of the bag?" he asked.

"If light shines on it the spirit will be able to escape," I explained.

He cocked his head to the side and turned up the corner of his mouth in a mocking smile of disbelief. Then he reached out his hand so he could feel the shape of the crystal through the bag.

"Look, everything else I've told you was true and I've proved it to you. Can't you believe me on this also? Just take my word for it, okay?" I pleaded.

He looked at me doubtfully for only a moment and finally said, "Okay." I breathed a big sigh of relief and smiled at him.

However, once I put the black bag back into my pocket the smile quickly melted from my face. I could feel the crystal vibrating slightly against my leg. I looked quickly at the others and wondered if I should say anything. My heart started pounding and I became nervous. William wanted out of the crystal.

CHAPTER 22

*J*ason left a very happy and excited person. He thanked my mother, Becky and me for a wonderful story. Even though he didn't say so, I felt that this story would be the beginning of a rise to the top for him. Mom went to take a shower and I seized that moment to approach Becky with the newest problem - the crystal.

"Tell me you're just making this up," Becky said with dread in her voice.

"I'm not. Here..." I pressed the bag into her hand, "feel this if you don't believe me."

She jerked her hand away as the bag plopped onto her bed and vibrated repeatedly. The movement it was making was getting stronger with every passing moment.

"What are we going to do?" she asked.

"Bury it," I stated.

"What? It's dark outside and freezing cold!" she complained.

"Would you rather have this thing in the house all night? God only knows what will happen while we're sleeping. Or would you rather bury it now while Mom is in the shower?" I was very blunt and there was no reason to sugar-coat the situation. Reluctantly, Becky agreed.

Dressed for the cold weather and armed with a shovel, the two of us tromped out into the dark pasture. I could feel the crystal in my pants pocket. Its movements had now become more of a violent jerking motion rather than a vibration. There was no way to tell if William was actually finding a way out of it or if he was just really mad.

"This ground is frozen," Becky complained.

"Let's just go closer to the stream. The ground will be a bit softer there," I suggested.

We dug a hole that was only knee deep but it would have to do because if I dug any deeper the water from the stream would come in and flood it, besides my fingers were frozen and I didn't want to stay out here too long.

"That's got to be good enough," Becky said out of breath. "And I'm sure Mom's finished with her shower and is wondering where we are."

"No she isn't. I left a note for her saying that we went to the barn to check on the animals," I said with my famous crooked smile.

"I thought you said we weren't going to keep lying?" Becky reminded me.

"This one was necessary," I came back quickly as I took the black bag out of my pocket. "He's really angry. I could feel this thing digging into my thigh the whole time we were working." I cupped the bag in my hands and dropped it into the hole. It hit the bottom with a thud.

"That's it then. Let's cover it up," Becky said. We didn't waste any time finishing the job; I shoveled and Becky push the dirt back into the hole.

Later that night as I lay in bed, I felt a wave of satisfaction. It was quiet in the house. The only sounds that could be heard were the wind and leaves blowing around outside. Of course the mice were running around inside the walls, but I was accustomed to them. Mom was actually sleeping in her bed instead of crashing on the sofa and Becky was already sound asleep. I let out a deep sigh of total relief and snuggled under my blankets. This was so much better - a normal house, nice and quiet.

I drifted off to sleep and started dreaming, at least it seemed like I had been dreaming. A sudden anxious feeling crept over me and I sat up in bed with a start and looked out my window toward the barn and the pasture. Hmmm that's funny, maybe it was my imagination but I could've sworn that I heard the sound of something sliding or being dragged on the ground out there.

I listened again. Nothing. Yeah, it had to be a dream...

About the Author

TJ Perkins is a gifted and well-respected author of mystery/suspense. A member of Sisters In Crime and The Maryland Writer's Association, her children's short stories have appeared in the Ohio State 6th Grade Proficiency Test Preparation Book, *Kid's Highway Magazine*, and Webzine 'New Works Review' with illustrations provided by Dennis Anfuso, just to name a few, and she's placed three times in the CNW/FFWA chapter book competition.

Finished works of her young reader's chapter books are entitled: The Fire and the Falcon (which won two chapter book awards), Wound Too Tight, Mystery of the Attic, On Forbidden Ground (all re-released under GumShoe Press May 2006), and books in the ongoing Kim & Kelly Mystery Series: Fantasies Are Murder, The Secret in Phantom Forest, Trade Secret, and Image in the Tapestry (which won a chapter book award), all with GumShoe Press March 2006.

About the Cover Designer

Paul Reynolds lives in Japan with his wife and colored pencils. Antisocial and encumbered with a debilitating sense of humor, Paul likes to draw unique things; claiming to strive for the beauty in ugliness. In reality, he just likes drawing ugly things because they tend to have more claws, teeth and wrinkles – and they're so much more fun! He draws most of the time and yet remains unproductive. Most of his illustrations are done with pencils on colored paper; some images are layered using digital software, but all are done slowly, meticulously and usually with no forward planning. Paul's formal art training is nonexistent. He has, however, been to a gallery. If you would like to contact Paul you are very welcome to do so via his website: www.eggman.co.nz.

About the Illustrator

Paul Salvi is a Baltimore-based writer, cartoonist, and illustrator. His screenplays have attracted the interest of agents and production companies; he stops doodling occasionally to pursue opportunities in film and publishing. See his work online at www.paulsalvi.com.

Printed in the United States
70551LV00001B/607-675

9 780977 753864